The SUNDOWN KID
A SOUTHWESTERN SHABBAT

by
Barbara Bietz

illustrated by
John Kanzler

August House, Inc.   Atlanta

Papa promised we would build a new life out West where the wide-open spaces were as big as the sky and the night stars shimmered so bright I could almost reach out, pull one down, and put it in my pocket.

Papa said we might be the only Jewish family in our desert town.

Mama promised some things would never change. She packed her silver candlesticks, Papa's kiddish cup, and her big soup pot.

After the long train ride, Sheriff Ryder greeted us.
"Howdy, neighbors." He tipped his hat.
"Howdy," I said and waved back.

Our adobe house stood alone on a hill.

A giant cactus guarded our front gate and colorful lizards darted inside and out.

Papa nailed a mezuzah on the doorway, making our house a home.

All week long I helped Papa clear space for planting.

Mama did our wash in a big metal tub, and I hung the clothes to dry in the sun.

I fed carrots to our horse, Clara, and climbed the biggest tree I could find. I imagined my cousin Izzy playing alongside me. "Yippe-ki-ay-a," I shouted like a real cowboy.

On Friday, Mama prepared for Shabbat. We bought flour to make challah from Mr. and Mrs. O'Toole at the general store.

Mama made a big pot of chicken soup, chock full of carrots and potatoes, just like always.

Papa took off his hat and put on a yarmulke.

I wore my best shirt and washed my face extra clean.

The smell of soup wrapped around me like a big hug from Mama.

There was a tapping outside. Did we have a visitor? Mama looked up with a start, like Uncle Morty or Aunt Lena would come waltzing in. But it was just the sagebrush, blowing against the window.

Before the sun set in the desert sky, Mama lit the candles.
Papa blessed the wine and the challah.
"Shabbat Shalom," Papa said and kissed my head.
Something didn't feel right.
"Too much soup," Mama said. "Not enough family."
The wide-open spaces were too big for Mama.

I had an idea. "Mama, next Shabbat why don't you make a very small pot of soup and a little bitty challah? Just enough for us!"

"I don't know how to make a small pot of soup," Mama said.

The next week, I helped Papa plant cotton seeds.

Mama made curtains for our windows.

I practiced spelling words on a slate board. Mama said I could write a letter to cousin Izzy.

Blacksmith Ricardo gave our Clara new shoes.

On Friday night, Papa took off his hat and put on a yarmulke.

I wore my best shirt and washed my face extra clean.

The smell of soup wrapped around me like a big hug from Mama.

There was a knocking noise at the door. Mama looked up with a start, like Cousin Shlomo or Aunt Goldie would come bouncing in. But it was just Clara, trying out her new shoes against the fence.

Before the sun set in the desert sky, Mama lit the candles.

Papa blessed the wine and the challah.

"Shabbat Shalom," Papa said and kissed my head.

Something didn't feel right.

"Too much soup," Mama said. "Not enough family."

"Oh, Mama," I said. "Who needs a big family on Shabbat? Remember how Izzy made such a mess slurping his soup?"

"Sweet Izzy. He loved my soup!" Mama sighed.

"How about Cousin Shlomo always wanting seconds?" I reminded her.

"Ah, Shlomo," Mama said. "He loved my soup!" Mama wiped her eyes.

"And Aunt Goldie? She asked for your recipe every week!" I said.

"Such a gem, Goldie. She loved my soup!" Mama held her face in her hands.

There was no talking Mama out of it.

Too much soup, not enough family.

I lost my appetite. Maybe the wide-open spaces were too big for me, too.

Sheriff Ryder stood outside the train station, greeting travelers.

"Howdy, neighbor." He tipped his hat.

"Howdy, Sheriff." I tipped my hat.

His shiny star-shaped badge looked like Mama's Jewish star necklace. Maybe we weren't the only Jewish family in town, after all!

I had an idea.

"Do you like chicken soup?" I asked.

"You betcha," he said. "Soup's a hearty meal."

Next I hopped over to Blacksmith Ricardo's workshop.

"Do you like chicken soup?" I asked.

"I do, little buckaroo!" Blacksmith Ricardo said.

I galloped to the general store.
"Do you like chicken soup?" I asked Mr. and Mrs. O'Toole.
"We love chicken soup!" they said at the very same time.
Mrs. O'Toole gave me a peppermint stick.

The wide-open spaces weren't big enough to hold my excitement. I skipped the whole way home.

On Friday night, Papa took off his hat and put on a yarmulke.

I wore my best shirt and washed my face extra clean.

The smell of soup wrapped around me like a big hug from Mama.

There was a knock at the door. Mama didn't even look up. But it was a REAL knock, not just sagebrush against the window or Clara trying out her new shoes.

In walked Sheriff Ryder and his wife, Mrs. Ryder.
"Howdy, neighbors." Sherrif Ryder tipped his hat.
Mrs. Ryder handed Mama a basket of wildflowers.

Next Blacksmith Ricardo came bouncing in. "Hi there, little buckaroo!" he said. Trailing behind Blacksmith Ricardo was a boy about my size. "This is my nephew, Miguel. He loves chicken soup, too!"

I gave Miguel the chair next to mine.

Finally, Mr. and Mrs. O'Toole waltzed in with their four little freckled O'Toole children. "We love soup!" they said at the very same time.

Our little adobe house was filled to the brim, just like Mama's soup pot!

Mama's smile was brighter than a cactus flower.

Before the sun set in the desert sky, Mama lit the candles.

Papa blessed the wine and the challah. Papa pulled off a big piece and passed it around for everyone to have a bite. I took two pieces and gave one to Miguel.

"Shabbat Shalom!" Papa said and kissed my head two times.

"Shabbat Shalom!" said our guests.

Mama filled bowl after bowl with hot chicken soup, heaped with vegetables.

The four freckled O'Tooles
slurped their soup, just like
Izzy but four times louder!

Sheriff Ryder asked for a second helping.

Mrs. O'Toole said, "I must have the recipe for this delicious soup!"

Mama served soup from the big pot until there wasn't a drop left, except for the carrot I saved for Clara.

Turns out the wide-open spaces were just
the right size for Papa, Mama, and me.

Author's Note

The setting of this story, the Wild West, has historical relevance. Many Jews settled in Western states in the 1800s and early 1900s and established businesses, schools, and synagogues. The communities were small and Jewish families were well integrated, living and working with non-Jewish families, while maintaining their religious values.

The act of welcoming guests, *hachnasat orchim*, is an important value in the Jewish community. In Genesis, Abraham's hospitality reflects his kindness when he invites strangers into his home and offers them a beautiful meal. Hachnasat orchim is a *mitzvah*, a good deed or commandment. Like many *mitzvot*, hospitality benefits both the giver and the receiver. In *The Sundown Kid*, the mama feels isolated and lonely. By inviting others to the Shabbat table, a sense of community is created for the family and the guests.

In loving memory of my mom and dad, who always had room at their table, in their home, and in their hearts. Much love.
—*BLB*

Many thanks to Diane and Lorelei,
who are with me in every painting.
—*JK*

Text © 2016 Barbara Bietz
Illustration © 2016 John Kanzler

Published 2016 by August House LittleFolk
augusthouse.com

Book Design by Graham Anthony

Printed by Pacom Korea

10 9 8 7 6 5 4 3 2 1   PB

LIBRARY OF CONGRESS CATALOGING-IN-PUBLICATION DATA

Names: Bietz, Barbara, author. | Kanzler, John, 1963- illustrator.
Title: The sundown kid : a southwestern shabbat / by Barbara Bietz ;
illustrated by John Kanzler.
Description: Atlanta : August House, Inc., 2016. | Summary: Shabbat is very
lonely for a boy and his parents when they move to a small town in the
"Wild West," until he begins asking townsfolk if they like chicken soup.
Identifiers: LCCN 2016013737 | ISBN 9781939160942 (pbk. : alk. paper)
Subjects: | CYAC: Jews--United States--Fiction. | Sabbath--Fiction. |
Hospitality--Fiction. | Moving, Household--Fiction. | West
(U.S.)--History--Fiction.
Classification: LCC PZ7.B4785 Sun 2016 | DDC [E]--dc23
LC record available at https://lccn.loc.gov/2016013737

011727K1/B0938/A6

The paper used in this publication meets the minimum requirements of the American National Standard
for Information Sciences— Permanence of Paper for Printed Library Materials, ANSI.48-1984